Fracture

The Complexity and the Human Learning Series

Books of a new bible for an emerging human species –
Homo adrians – one finally deserving of its stablely fluid
and simply complex, or paradoxical, mind.

Frontispiece

It doesn't matter if they ever believe I was possible. (It doesn't matter how far Adrian+Patrick ever became possible.) What's important is that they someday soon ascend into the immersion of many more, if not all, of their possibilities.

Copernicus again

Fracture

a 12:2 hyp

Copernicus again

Veronica + Jennifer –
Thanks for making history
and art.

Copernicus again

Writers Club Press
San Jose New York Lincoln Shanghai

Fracture
a 12:2 hyp

Published by Writers Club Press
an imprint of iUniverse.com, Inc.

For information address:
iUniverse.com, Inc.
620 North 48th Street
Suite 201
Lincoln, NE 68504-3467
www.iuniverse.com

Front Cover Art Credit by Adrston

ISBN: 0-595-00224-2

Printed in the United States of America

Dedication

To Louis Niebur,

for the inspiration and the sweetness

and for Adrian "dreamboy" Johnston

I do not know what it is about you
that closes and opens;
only something in
me understands the voice of your eyes
is deeper than all roses

ee cummings

and for SEK,

always

Epigraph

We need to use the brains in our heads.

AAJ

There is neither Jew nor Greek, there is neither slave nor free, there is neither male nor female; for you are all one...

Jesus of Nazareth

It's not trespassing when you cross your own boundaries.

Copernicus again

What did you think joy was,
some slight and ordinary thing?

Copernicus again

Fracture

...and we look toward the waitress thinking she must be the woman we saw dance on a theater stage that afternoon in New York when we passed the quivering purplous flowers of wisteria heaped against the wrought-iron rail enclosing a church on Twenty-First Street, and thought how this was what we were supposed to discover in great cities:

a wall of flowers amid this steel, this should settle and diminish our misery—but it didn't, we raced on, fabulously fractured, amazed that the obvious and persistent formula—perception into transform-mation—produced no results, did not engage us; so we ran on.

Charlie Smith
Perception One
Indistinguishable from the Darkness

prologue

I've scored again. This is easier than I thought. They keep getting more and more beautiful. Kal, Clifton, Craig, Adam, David, Louis.

I didn't think anyone would ever top Kal. But Craig blew him away. And then Louis shattered that record. Why did I think it was so hard? What was it that frightened me? How easily he climbed into my bed. Michael.

Did he pull me there?

I want someone to make me whole.

Pause, into a few seconds of silence. Reflect. Revise. This is important. Tantamount.

No, scratch that. ~~want~~ Make it need. Underline that: <u>need</u>.

Emphasize the word with your inflection.

Keep it *someone. Something* will no longer do.

I need *someone* to make me whole. There. That is better.

Repeat this to yourself. Make it your mantra. This is not a train of thought you want to mention to anyone else. As if they would care.

They might care too much for your own good. Maintain the repetition, slow it down to melody. And keep trying; don't stop looking.

kaleidoscope

We try to balance our glasses of wine. I jostle him slightly, repositioning ourselves. A small slurp of grape juice sloshes over the lip of my glass. A burgundy flower blooms on the linen. It turns yellowish on the blue sheets.

He moves to wipe it up. I grab his hand to say that it doesn't matter. He stops. We look into each other's eyes and see more important things on our minds.

The wine glasses are over one hundred years old, I tell him. Hand blown by my great-grandfather and given to me by my his son's wife. This impresses him.

"Just don't break them," I tease with some seriousness.

He understands how irreplaceable they are.

"Maybe we shouldn't use them," he suggests.

"They can't sit all the time collecting dust on a shelf," I tell him. "I need to get some use out of them."

Life has to be lived, I think; we are not goblets to be viewed in a museum exhibition.

We set the wine aside. From that motion it is a quick transition to shedding the clothes of our day and re-dressing by sliding next to each other under the covers. The hot humid days have retreated at the chill of an approaching cold front. A brisk August night slips in through an open window along with sounds of traffic squealing around the corner. Revelers walking into the night and down to the bar district shout their music that filters in with the breeze. His body is a furnace that warms me. I feel the gusts of hot air with each exhalation.

In a whisper that draws me close he says, "so tell me about yourself." I ask him, "what do you want to know?" He says, "everything."

"Everything? Where do you want me to start?"

"At the beginning," he answers.

He wants me to name every boyfriend I've ever had, starting with the very first. And I should leave no one out. Does he count? I would like to ask him. He wants to know my passions, my desires, every dream. I plead, that's a tall order.

For clarification, to stall, to reduce the stakes, I ask him again, where I should begin? He says, at the first moment of memory, whatever flash my imagination could recall. His smile reassures me. His arms squeeze me tight with a seriousness I had not expected.

"I know we just met," he says, "but it seems I know a lot about you."

He says he had talked about me at length with his friends. He recounts the times he had seen me walking along the streets. Once I paused to look in the window of a bookstore. He was inside looking back, unnoticed. "Oh, I noticed," I tell him. And there was that night of my birthday he saw me at the Hungarian Bistro with Louis. He sat with friends at a table across the room. When the waiter brought my cake, he describes for me, and the whole restaurant sang "Happy Birthday," he sang the loudest. When I blew out the candles, he made a wish. He kisses me on the cheek. The wish has come true.

For all this, he tells me, he thought this relationship might become special, even though it hasn't yet begun. "You know the kind where we get to know each other so well we could not ever be separated." I nod. "Oh!," his face tightens, "I mean that's not what I'm thinking. I am not obsessed." I nod again.

Unbelievably, I did not think I was his obsession. What he said had plausibility. The most absurd come-on lines never entered my mind. But someone had lit a sparkler inside my chest and was swirling it around in the black night. The erratic orange trails of light circled the folded-over flaps of my brain.

"So start talking," he laughs. His determination grabs me low. He holds firmly, with a tug—his emphasis we need to move on quickly to other things.

What should I tell him? The truth? And how much of it? How would I fill in the gaps? There were so many. The truth would be very sparse, convoluted, disconnected, ripped open wide with numerous and growing holes. My life was a connect-the-dots, most of the points so unrelated. Even if someone had drawn lines among all of them, there would be no decipherable design. Did he want to know the pain or just the good? The times of joy would be short, and we could get down to business. The tales of hurt would take forever, but at least they'd be interesting. How would I explain the breaks, the endless wearing of casts upon my spirit? I was on a first name basis at the emergency room of the soul. I had the VIP card of rejection and loneliness. And what life would I give him—the one I know, or the one I wanted? Or the one that I lived in most of the time: whatever I happened to make-up to get through to the next hour of existence?

I knew I could astound him with my dreams. They would turn his infatuation for me into love. Let's hope he didn't soon meet my friend, Steve, who once cruelly joked to me with an ironic truth, "That's Scott, always one step away from his dreams." Maybe I would give him everything. That's what he asked for.

He seemed sincere. Doesn't someone who cares about you take the good with the bad—even if the bad lasts for a winter of dark, and the good is such a fleeting spring that when it's over you can't be sure the light wasn't something hallucinatory or imagined? I'd give him my all.

Maybe my friend Adam was right to believe in destiny. This encounter was meant to be. Sitting in my bed, listening to the stories he requested, he'd find some redeeming value, filter through all my wild cantonations—my concocted realities, my sad, sad themes—and tell me what I could no longer do for myself: tell me what was real for me and what was not. And all this would please him.

He encouraged me, did he not? You heard him ask for it all. Remember he said this felt so special. Wasn't he prepared?

We melt into one another. The digital clock clicks intermittently, a back beat to my oral history. He still holds me tight, still smiles. My audience of one. My greatest fan.

"Speak to me. Tell me who I am loving." Tell me who I am loving for the rest of my life.

Isn't this too much to go through for what is likely to be just a one night stand?

"Tell me," he says, a desperation shadowing his voice, as if I were the one starting to pull away. As if I were betraying something so fixed and old and yet only a few hours into its bubbling up to the surface where it might crystallize into form before first evaporating. "Tell me," he purrs. And at that moment he seems the very embodiment of trust, something that...

He pulls down my jaw, sticks an index finger to my tongue. In play he massages my Adam's apple. "Sing, I command you." I open my mouth.

With the push of his fingers words roll forth from my lips, spilling onto the blankets—like gold nuggets rolling along in a mountain stream. He is a prospector picking every one up and plunking them in his copper pan. Iced cold water drains through the pie-tin's holes. A scant oiliness rises off the pebbles and creates a surface film in which forms a rainbow of refraction. He marvels at the color. I open my mouth, and this is what I tell him.

partum

The glare of light pierces into scream; a howl. People on the street below cover their ears and hurry away. Floating in the warm puddingocean of blood, the ripples push me forward, sturgeons swimming past me, fins propelling my torso into a canal, a ribbed narrow passage in the underwater cave, the exit to air and blue and bright.

She cries and clenches the table, her wound hole gaping, glistening with the puckered smile of a starlet, beckoning moisture, murky seaweed films of red. This one is special, she thinks. More so than the rest. This one, genius.

Knives ripping at her flesh, dark alley, sear her into pieces. "No. No. Please. Don't. Stop. You're hurting me. Here, take my purse. Please. There's money inside. Take as much as you want. Take it all." Freight train to the head, falling, falling to the bed.

Hard cobblestone her pillow. A blunt object pings next to her body. Once, twice, then rings silent, still, swallowed by her oozing body fluid. In this I swim, a tadpole in this tidal pool. My eyes open. Lungs inflating with the world rushing in.

"My boy. My precious boy." Not like the others. Blessed. Worth the pain. This she whimpers.

She pulls me from the blood, from the men and women in green suits, criminals with matching masks. Blood drips off of me like water from a shower, swirling to the floor drain that does not exist, until a stream forms, a brook of my blood, and it leaps its banks and spatters everyone's shoes. It drips and flows and turns into a river of murdered lives. This woman who calls herself my mother holds me high in her hands and I see the landscape as a relief map—the river widened by many tributaries.

One hundred priests use aluminum softball bats of words to cave in the skulls of homosexuals, right below Mary's triumphant eyes. The metal dents but does its job. Parishioners crowd forward soaking their Sunday best in the bloody streams and their tongues in the overflowing communion cups. The fumes from the factory next door to the church waft in and shroud the church-goers' parallel actions.

Men in Nazi regalia push Jews live into ovens. A celebration service. Dark ones and outsiders are used to stoke the flames. As always. The 1940s continue to burn, the grease soots the air, soiling the pressed immaculate uniforms, coloring them into U.S. ones, pushing young men and women onto the poison fields of Iraq. She laughs, smothers me with joy.

She holds me in her arms, rocking. She babbles.

This drama of human kindness continues before me. Each reel of the tape played from the beginning through the unlearned future, and rewound and shown again. Corpses choke the river. My mother is hysterical and being restrained. The nurses hold her down. Black-gloved hands circle her throat, pushing deeper into her neck than her own trachea. She gurgles, barely. Her damaged hair a cushion against the brick. She squirms slightly. The doctor holds me up, pink and wrinkled and the most frightening sight—if one were not told to think exactly the opposite. I wriggle upside down in the freedom of the firm, brown, female m.d. hands.

I watch this battered woman from this vantage point. Her body shakes. It trembles. I would comfort her were I not so small. The word "messiah" comes out of her mouth smoothly, amidst the convulsions, again and again. What kind of vision is this? The picture of Mary begins to cry. Christ's wooden stigmata drip opiatic blood. Who is this woman on the table? One person in green soils her pants at the answer.

Then another. The stench rises. Someone has come. Is come. This horror empties everyone's bowels.

Yellow glare flashes on white. A blue burst blinds. I open my mouth and spit out blood, spit out the cum and vaginal pus of the Nazis now born in Cincinnati, the Sieg Heil transformed to genuflection or the tirades of an anti-abortionist.

This woman who calls herself my mother loses her grip on me. I do not fall to the pavement but bounce upwards upon the operatic bombasts issued from her lungs; sounds the hospital staff cannot restrain, decibels that are echoed in her hairy-black cavern. I am nineteen years old and in his arms.

His ass is hairy. (What a fantastic, slender sight from behind.) From this view his balls hang down, the size of small lemons. He licks the blood from my mouth. The teeth shine. This woman flails her arms at me, strikes at the separation. But I am no longer hers. Into the world's night I turn my face. His strong arms hold me.

"He will be special," she stutters. Sedatives fog the room, but this statement to her has the clarity of rain on a freshly waxed car, the peeking sun dancing in each scurrying bead. "He will never again be mine, but he will be remembered."

I do not know his name. His tongue is sweet and his hair short and spiked, dark as the fur between this woman's legs. I want to ask his name. So that I might remember. So that I might look him up. But that is part of the deal. This experience is given to me only if I keep it anonymous, only if it is so far inside my mind that he does not even sense our encounter. What to pay to put a ring of platinum on his finger, to meet him in the gym and play badminton until we're sweaty and in need of showering.

Not, anyway, in this world—this darkness that can barely anticipate light.

I am strong and raised. She is a wisp of smoke, fading. The shadow of my face grows larger; it chills her presence. Her cracked lips part to speak my name, to smile as her arms reach for me. I never knew her. Deep into this night of unremembrance she is frozen, teeth locked in the satisfied smile of a parent, the child returned home for the holiday.

I do not know her name, my mother. The badged woman tells me she was once important to me. How do I embrace this body, smudged and ripped to shreds? Raped and impregnated and robbed. Lying there stiffly, waiting for the police to save her, to bury her, easing her down into a gentleness that is entirely alien. Through the mascara of dried blood I kiss her cheek. I touch her bony shoulder. If only out of politeness, this is my goodbye. I do not know his name, and I lie there patiently, wrapped around him, wishing the morning sun would not ever again decide to rise.

Without our glasses we are blind each in other's mouth. We press against each other, we press into each other. Our organs, his larger than mine, become one giant siamese twin, joined at the friction.

Someone sounds at the door, some one pumps bullets into the door, screaming "faggot." Words launching holes in the wall, into the sofa on which we couple, our bodies matted together, sweaty chests and leg hair intertwined. Visions of these atrocities pelt my face, the plaster explodes from the barrage. A bullet rips through my lung, bits of which I cough onto him. Pink and slimy, resting on his chest, like a newborn resting on its mother.

He holds my hand. I open my mouth. She reaches for me. It's all before me now. The river of blood is swollen. Who does it not contain? I slide from her into his caress. Why can't I stay with you?, I ask him. Don't leave me, she begs. This is my birth. I open my mouth and into the light I scream.

fracture

On my tenth birthday the best gift I received was a kaleidoscope. It was wrapped in gold paper and delivered by my friend Joshua, who lived next door. The present actually came from my entire Little League baseball team. I was our league's batting champion. My fourteenth home run belted us into the playoffs and earned us a trip to Minneapolis. Joshua came to my room to show me how to use my new toy; by peering through the length of its tube into the corona of any ordinary light bulb. I aimed it at the ceiling light above my desk. With each turn of my wrist the fragments of colored glass created new universes of patterns—each which I thought were like snowflakes; someone new to love, unique, never existed before, likely not to ever exist again.

The best way, Joshua said, was to look through the scope at the sun. The colors were always the brightest, the patterns most brilliant. It was how you got the purest effect. The designs you saw gave you your money's worth. And it was worth a lot of money, to kids in the sixth grade. Twelve dollars, divided up among eighteen team members. Each one had gladly contributed his share.

I glanced over to Josh to show my appreciation for his suggestions. He had lain down on my bed. The top of his pants were wrapped around his knees. He was stroking himself into the biggest erection I had ever seen. The only one besides my own.

"I have my own kaleidoscope," he joked. "Didn't cost me nothing. I can play with it anytime. And when I close my eyes and stroke it, I see really neat designs."

"Which do you think is more fun?" he said. "Your toy or this?"

When I took what little of it that could be slid into my mouth and closed my eyes, I saw precisely what he promised. The patterns rotating and twisting and designed in my head were far more exciting than anything I could view peering down the length of that wooden tube.

Still, I played with my gift, and I played with Josh, all summer long. I even went so far as to carry the toy in my gym bag. During slow innings of games I would take it out and gaze on the mass of the crowd. Their collective form absorbed the light and dulled the reflection in the prism. The muted design was always different from looking into bright light, sometimes a variance just what I preferred.

Josh already had hair, and he always like to point out to me that it was the same color as that on his head. "I'm a natural brunette," he would laugh at the absurdity of his own joke. Once he went to a costume store and got some hair dye to make it green. "Just to shock you," he confessed, as if it was a special present. I was the only one he ever did things like this with.

Then summer was ending and we would be returning to the gang showers at school. He wanted to stand out. One day in my bedroom, my mom downstairs baking chocolate chip cookies, I sprayed shaving cream on his genitals and carefully shaved him bald. Not a nick. And he rewarded me with the longest kiss I had ever had. It could have lasted into the fall when we entered junior high and saw less of each other; he opting for football and I staying with the autumn baseball season. And our relationship continued in a way. Only late at night could we get together, to study, just the two of us. We weren't really boyfriends. We were just together. And everybody knew about us.

Well, not everybody. But enough. Too many for our own good.

Junior high was different. Students from a confluence of elementary schools flowed into one large and primarily foreign student body. Most of the boys on our baseball team I did not recognize, not even from the public leagues. Like Larry and Pete— two ninth graders who asked me to stay after practice and play catch. Then in the dugout, when everyone else had left, they exposed themselves to me.

When I touched Larry, thinking he would be as sincere as Josh, the word "Fag" slammed against the side of my head, followed by one fist and then another. The leggings of my uniform got twisted around my legs as I was de-pantsed and pushed to the ground. They began an experiment to see if a bat could be inserted into my anus.

"Is this how you like to be fucked?," Pete taunted.

The contents of my gym bag bounced in the dirt around my face as Larry emptied it. My kaleidoscope fell into the mud, dirt moistened by the blood draining from my nose. Larry picked it up and laughed. Ingenuous as he was, he pleased himself with his discovery of a new sex toy for me.

This wooden member was so large. They soon tired of the frustration of insertion, or lack there of. Larry slammed it against the edge of the dugout bench. The glass shattered and the colorful shards spilled into the dirt. They sparkled in the light as Larry and Pete ran away.

I coughed and sputtered and struggled to my feet and went home to Josh's. He got me to his room unseen, and I called my parents and asked permission to stay the night. A tough sell on a Wednesday. Josh's parents agreed on his word alone. They did not come to his room to verify I was there. The next morning my nose would be black but the swelling would have gone down. I could face my parents with some excuse that evening. Some idea would come to mind. I left the kaleidoscope in the dugout. My parents had forgotten about it. They wouldn't know it was missing. Josh snuck out to retrieve it. He found the many fragments of glass scattered in the dust. The moon was full and sparked the pieces to light with its powerful shine. In the black of the dugout they looked like a sky full of stars, lit up brightly, but not white as normal, rather every possible color. Josh picked up as many as he could, dropped them in the tube and hurried home.

That night I dreamed my nose was healed and I awoke to walk to the craft gallery to buy a brand new kaleidoscope, more magnificent than the first one. A mahogany tube and gold-plated fittings. Pride illuminated me when I got it home and pointed it at the sun. I remember that it was polished too well and slipped from my hands. The force of it hitting the floor cracked it wide open, and all the particles of glass spilled out and flowed quickly away from me like the rage of a flood-swollen river. In my dream, I tried frantically to pick up all the pieces.

shards-8

We were just kids. It was all supposed to be make believe. No one was supposed to even get hurt. Really. It was just a game.

The boys in my brother's sixth grade class pulled the beard off the man who was playing Santa Claus to prove he was make-believe. Their action, however, prompted a decision that upper level classes would no longer get a visit from Santa. Only Mrs. Claus would entertain them. Santa would only visit the younger levels, like my kindergarten class. We didn't believe in Santa either. I knew Santa did not exist. I had walked by the principal's office earlier in the day and saw the husband of the school nurse standing in the office foyer pulling on the red velvet suit. Still, my class had high enough stakes in the game to play by the rules.

When I climbed onto Santa's lap I'm sure I asked for something faddish, materialistic, expensive. Perhaps a guitar or an electric train set. A classmate of mine asked for a gun. Santa balked at this request, but on Christmas morning we found he had honored this same wish for my older brother and his friends.

The best thing about my older brother was that he did not treat me like a younger one. He was not embarrassed or irritated to have me hang around him, to follow him and his friends on their frequent excursions into the woods. There they had built a clubhouse and sometimes were allowed to spend the night, drinking pop, sometimes beer, eating snacks, and looking at their stash of Playboys with the shine of a flashlight. It was here they practiced kissing one another, to get ready for girls. It was here they watched each other test themselves. Their slender torsos would arc in the air and their naive erections would twist, but nothing shot across the room except their pantomimes. My brother gave me presents, took me to the soda fountain for toasted bagels and Cherry Cokes. My brother asked me to go walking with his friends on the day that I would come back home without him.

It was spring, a hint of winter still blasted at our jackets months after the guys had ripped the wrapping off their .410 shotguns on Christmas day. A charge of electricity in the breeze sparked new life and invigorated all that was already there. We walked through the woods, the trees ornamented in a scant dusting of green, budding leaves barely starting to protrude. I watched my brother and his friends shoot at rabbits, which sprinted off dazed, disturbed, but unharmed. I watched as they played this game "Executioner's Song." My brother, taken pretend prisoner-of-war, was made to kneel before the others on his knees. His two classmates pronounced his verdict of "guilty" and sentenced him to death. It was just a game. The two both aimed their guns at him. In make believe they pulled the triggers, "POECCCHHH," mimicking the explosion of their guns. We were just kids. No one ever got hurt.

One of his friends got carried away. His finger accidentally slipped and the trigger collapsed for real. My brother squealed, the force of the point blank shot slamming his face into the dirt.

"What are you doing?" I screamed. I got no answer.

The first shot seemed to break all barriers. Everything spun out of control. I watched friend number two fire a shot into the back of my brother's neck. I watched in horror, backing away, as this began to excite them.

I kept retreating, walking backwards up a slight incline, taking two or three nervous steps, getting farther and farther away, each time they pumped another shell into his head. My brother stopped squirming, became still and silent. They did not stop, though, until they were out of ammunition and the face of my sibling was no longer recognizable.

They looked down upon his body and they shook. They shook with fear. Tears began rolling down their faces. Then they started to laugh. I heard his ribs crack when they jumped up and down on him. Their laughter turned into sounds that I had not ever heard before, like some animal that had long been contained suddenly released from its prison. Their sounds ripped through me and made me tremble as well.

Then they stopped. It became very quiet. And they turned around and looked at me.

Fortunately I had put fifty or so feet between us in my back-peddling. Sensing their intentions and hearing, "We have to get him. He'll squeal. The little queer." I fled out of the woods with the two of them in hot pursuit. I sped through the woods, branches slapping my face and underbrush slashing my shins. Terror making me fly. I broke into the open, the meadow, and flew to the edges of our subdivision where their chase would become conspicuous and stifled and I could fall into the protection of civilization. My screams would be heard.

I never would have made it. The sprint to safety was at least two miles long. We always walked quite a ways. My head start was not that great. Save for murderer one tripping and severely spraining his ankle, with murderer two stopping to help him, the police would have found me in those woods, instead of the two thugs, my body, silent, still, not far from my brother's.

Without a chance in hell, I ran anyway. I ran as fast as I could, faster than ever before, past my house, out of my neighborhood, into areas I did not know. I kept running until I was exhausted, until the ground pulled me down hard, slugging the wind out of my lungs. I collapsed. Then I kicked and screamed from my hands and knees and pounded that damned earth. I pounded until my fists ached. I pounded until my lungs racked with the searing burning of my constant screaming. I stopped and caught my breath, resting. As I lay on my stomach, my chest, in and out, rapidly, pushed the ground beneath it to its molten core. Dirt was sucked in with each breath. Into my mouth, up my nostrils. The grains of soil melting on my tongue. I choked and coughed as I swallowed it. As soon as I was able I got up and I ran some more.

From that point forward, it never stopped. From my days as a six-year old, my legs were always in motion, pumping and churning. I had to shower constantly to wash off the sweat. I fantasized about being able to suck in the breaths with an oxygen mask permanently attached to my face. I got into great shape.

Running, running, running—past my parents with their shocked faces, under the legs of the men with badges who came to my house and didn't stop asking questions, around and between the red-eyed relatives who visited us in droves and whispered to each other behind cupped hands, "Poor child, he doesn't seem to be understanding any of this." I ran through my brother's funeral, kicking and screaming. I pounded on his casket. I wanted it open. I wanted to kiss good-bye his face that was no longer a face. I pounded some more till my father swooped me up in his arms and quieted me in an anteroom. It felt good in his grasp, a cradle I never wanted to leave. When I calmed down and he let me go, I dropped to the floor and I started pounding again. This time I pounded on me.

I pummeled myself when I sat in the classroom. I did it harder when I was sent to the principal's office, or worst yet to the counselor's. I pummeled myself so hard that the bruises on my body became like moles and birthmarks—permanent, in the right light, almost alluring. I beat myself so hard that my parents were questioned for child endangerment. I felt guilty for the hushed accusations they had to endure on Sunday mornings in church or whenever they went into the public for something as mundane as grocery shopping, but I kept on abusing myself anyway.

I learned this trick where I could slide safety pins under the skin of my forearms, lock them in their clasps and pull. I was a candy maker stretching taffy, ripping the flesh open, until my arms became swollen and white with pus, until I was hospitalized for infection and restrained, my limbs wrapped in heavy gauze. The doctor came in to unwrap the bandages and inspect my wounds. My mother fainted and my father's knees buckled at the sight of the reddened tracks that scarred me as if they were part of some ancient initiation ritual. I remember smiling for the first time since that spring day. I think I remember saying the word "cool," and the doctor almost slapping me for it, and my mother crying as if she had just lost another son.

My parents had to send me away to juvenile homes. To wherever the next best solution was. Yet no matter where I was placed I kicked and screamed until I escaped. They would always find me and bring me back. And I would always kick and scream against their efforts. Even under heavy sedation, during my frequent stays at our community hospital's psychiatric ward, my conscious convulsions continued. I broke free from my restraints, crashed through a window, and kept on running. The glass lacerating my body, left a bloody trail of breadcrumbs that was easy enough to follow, but still, I kept running. And I kept one step ahead of them. No one could match my endurance.

I ran through my parents divorce; a marriage soured from the trauma of one son murdered and the other turned psycho. I ran until I was fourteen and could take no more. I ran while playing coy to the truck drivers who—one-by-one—took me farther west, allowing me to sleep in their cabs and shower with them in the facilities at truck stops, where they bought me my meals, thinking they were winning my trust so they could call the authorities and notify my parents. I ran while they thought I was still in the booth. They were on the phone giving the police my description as a possible runaway youth that was sought back in Michigan. I slipped right past them, the metallic phone cord dangling nervously in their hands. I would be on the interstate and into a car before they had finished the conversation. I had long since ceased being under anyone's control.

I grew and developed, my body started to fill out and muscles became larger. I found I could run faster and harder and longer. Had I been in high school instead of a drop-out I would have won state in cross-country. I ran harder and harder and harder, faster and faster and faster, longer and longer and longer. I kept thinking if I could just push myself a little bit more, a little bit more, I could run so fast and so far away that I would break free of this ugly life that held me like a helpless mouse in the talon's of a hawk. I could leave my competitors in my wake, the finishing line ribbon trailing around my hips, flowing behind me like a bridal train. I would run right out of the stadium, not even bothering to pick up my trophy. I would run until I got all the way to Los Angeles, a new life in its freedom, where I could lose myself in the big city. If that were not enough, I would run into the ocean, plowing into those waters full force, until the waves swept me off my feet, blanketing over me, smothering me in a slumber I had not known for years, sucking me into a void where brothers are not killed with Christmas presents, where childhood is not shattered as easily as pulling off Santa's fake beard. I would run and run and run until I got there. To safety. To quiet. Just to there. *Wherever.* Sitting across from my brother, sipping on a Cherry Coke through a straw, munching on the crispness of a bagel, hot butter dripping down my chin.

shards-124

"What did you do to get in here?"

I tell them, "I don't belong here." I tell them how I don't deserve to be in this place, that I made one mistake that was only partially my fault; and I was a victim of an epochal, hysterical bloodlust for law and order; that I really was on my way to medical school. Hell, right now, I should be a practicing physician, a respected member of the community.

They toss their heads back in a laugh and chortle, "Yeah, right." Their laugh is a good one.

Though I'm not matched for this environment, I'm no pushover. I've established my ground—even learned to tolerate sex with other men. Sometimes, actually, I seek it out. We all need a little companionship and affection in this place, but I won't be raped.

That happened to me several times when I first came. Now I'm quite good at fashioning knives out of utensils or whatever I can find and I can hold my own. People know my reputation. They call me "The Cutter" because I won't think twice about slicing someone who tries to force himself on me. When my weapons get taken away I just make more. Now with this Lorena Bobbit thing, I want the word to get out that I won't hesitate doing what she did, either. Except it won't be retrievable. It will be flushed down the toilet, or taken to the kitchen and put in the meat grinder.

If these people want to think I'm wacko, that's fine. They will leave me alone, which is what I usually want—to be by myself, to count the days, stay on good terms, not do anything to damage my review when I come up for my next parole hearing.

There are moments in my cell, when I lay on my bed that hangs from the gray wall and I fantasize. They let me bring in a TV and a recliner, and I got to hang up some art posters, fastened of course with Scotch tape, not push pins, to break up this monotony. The recessed, grilled flourescent lights hum overhead. Next cell I can hear poker being played. Most men, I suppose, would fantasize throwing the winning touchdown in the last seconds of the Super Bowl, or perhaps sinking their dicks again into the soft, grabbing folds of a pussy. Some even torture themselves by thinking about freedom, getting out of this joint, breathing the air, under the sky; discovering that its blueness extends beyond the guarded walls of a courtyard.

I dream of something different. A twenty-one-year-old man is brought into my emergency room—run down in the middle of an intersection. Walking against a red light. Taunting a car flowing with the green. Daring its driver to hit him. Stopping in the intersection to test his macho, primitive urge. His legs have suffered multiple fractures. Contusions and abrasions leopard spot his body; a result of the automobile slamming him to the asphalt, flipping and dragging him for over ten feet. Barely conscious, he has a concussion. There is significant blood loss and signs of internal bleeding. To put it mildly, he is quite a mess. If anything bright can be said of his accident, it is that it occurred so near to the trauma center I happen to head.

I cannot share the medical jargon I need to describe the procedures I would enact over the next few critical hours because in real-life I never made it this far. I only received my letter of acceptance to medical school two weeks before I was arrested and eventually sent to prison. But in layman's terms, this is what I would do: His legs would be set. Surgery would be performed to repair his ruptured internal organs. And though he would not return to a condition as good as new, he would recover almost fully, with only a slight barely noticeable hitch in his gait. The Veritas University Hospitals & Clinics's Trauma Center was not named one of the top five in the country by *U.S. News & World Report* by accident. Most certainly he would not have died, and perhaps the driver who hit him would have been charged only with something minor—like "failure to yield to a pedestrian"—and not "attempted murder," which was upgraded to "homicide" when the pedestrian died a few days later.

The intriguing part of this story is that the driver was not even drunk. He ought to have been in full control, and the student crossing the street was brilliantly illuminated in the car's headlights. It could have been daylight. Thus it was not a case of the driver not seeing the student—apparently it was the exact opposite.

His friends who crossed with him, on their way downtown to meet some buddies at a bar, knew enough to get out of the way, to run to the safety of the sidewalk. The student, however, played up his rudeness, if you will, as if he ruled the road, daring the driver with his hesitation. What possessed either one of them at that moment has never been satisfactorily answered. All that is known is he slowed his step and when the automobile accelerated, he stopped and locked his eyes with its sole occupant.

All games have rules, even this one. The way this contest of inconsiderations was supposed to have played out, the driver should have slowed down or swerved out of the way. The pedestrian should have followed his friends and leaped to the curb. But that didn't happen. The car plowed right through him, drove over him, as if he were a dandelion in a buffalo stampede.

When the vehicle came to a stop, thirty yards away, and the driver's eyes looked into the rearview mirror and saw the motionless body on the ground—the blood not yet having time to drain and pool—with the student's dazed and wet-cheeked friends huddled over him, I clenched the rubber padding of the steering wheel, hard, until the pressure made permanent indentations, and I shook.

I shook, but I did not necessarily feel sorry.

shards-102

"I can't believe someone stole my fucking towel."

"I had my swimsuit stolen once. I don't know who would be hard up enough to do that. It surely didn't fit him, with my waist size being so small. I bet he was one of those guys with a fetish. You know, he smelled them while he whacked himself off. Or he'd lay on top of them, feeling the smoothness, the coolness of the fabric, while he dry humped the bed. And it wasn't just the fact that swimsuits were expensive that annoyed me. That pair had sentimental value. They were signed by Mark Spitz."

"Oh they were not!...Here, put this in your mouth. You talk too much, and I can't believe any of your stories."

Before he complied with my request, he put an index finger to the two inch segment of raised skin just below my right rib cage. Its pinkness glistened as he rubbed his finger over it. My worm, I called it, for it could resemble such that is found littering a rainy day sidewalk.

"Do you think it will ever go away?" he asked with his soft blue eyes.

"No, the doctor says it will pretty much stay the way it is now. I'll always have it…a reminder of your love."

He looked down, wanting to shrink from the room.

That two inch deformity of skin was like our wedding band.

For him, a constant source of regret, something he had to forever make up for. He would not ever get over how easily he slid the knife into my flesh or how the sound and the feel of the rip sickened him, forcing him to recoil-but only briefly-before he bent over me, profusely screaming how sorry he was. Knife dropped to the floor, no wits about him, hands to his head.

"Just get me a towel," I said. "Just get me to the hospital," I screamed back at him.

For me, this uneven ridge was a source of leverage; something I could always hold over his head. *You aren't going to stab me again, are you?* I'd use to disarm him. Or *Why don't you just knife me? That would hurt far less?*

It was our mutual bond that neither one of us could ever let go of. And it was what we used to not ever let go of one other.

Now he quivered in my arms, having sunk his body next to mine in an attempt to appease his guilt. His warmth blanketed me. "You don't know how sorry I am. Really. I—"

"Yes, I do. You know you're forgiven."

"And forgotten!" His innocence was showing.

"Oh, I didn't say forgotten."

"Then I can't be forgiven if you can't forget it."

"Let's not start this again," I said, trying to relax against this new source of tension. "What about putting this in your mouth. Let's let bygones be bygones."

"Yeah, we have each other." Spoken like a true putti. "That's all that matters."

He startled me by licking my three-month-old lovers'-quarrel wound—gently, all the way from the bottom to the top, in one smooth, extended motion. It tingled. Then he zig zagged his tongue quickly down the ridge. Electricity shivered my body. A new version of foreplay. Then he did it again. I lay stunned.

He looked at me, laughed, and buried his face into my request.

I placed my palm on the bright red hair of his scalp, laying my hands upon his effort. Then I touched the knobby scar. His tongue had left it moist, lubricated—a shaft in its own right, ready to massage.

I moved my fingers up and down it, kneading it. slowly, gently at first, as if I was nervously twirling a ring about my finger. Though I was wholly at peace. Then I increased the pace and the intensity until I fell into a rhythm that matched the bobbing of his head.

shards-19

"Do you want me to tell you the secrets of the universe?"

"No, not you again. Go away. Please, leave us alone."

shards-78

Sleep coaxes me from death. The .357 – which I keep loaded in the only drawer of my bedside stand as my guarantee that anytime I choose I can make the pain go away – waits patiently for another night. Morning will erase the surface despair, but underneath some of my life's resilience will have been sapped. And it's been more than a few years since this has started to show.

God, how I wish I could write like this in my journal, in the same eloquent manner I think. Then people would be attracted to my writing. But instead of *sleep coaxes me from death,* however, or *morning will erase surface despair,* I get this:

Ran only about two miles. Saw this hot karate guy in a towel.

Called Steve last night. He was out of his room, and I was on my way out the door, so I didn't get to talk to him.

But here is one pearl I wrote: *The concept of evil is an arbitrary one...and it often turns out to be something that rises above the established limits on imagination, courage, or excellence.*

Well, that's not so good but this one is better: *I believe people were born good, of their own accord. It was only later that they developed religion and patriotism to convince themselves of that or to persuade themselves otherwise.*

That one's not so bad, but when I show this writing to others, the tension over the hatred to my words sucks the air right out of our lungs. Or so I have experienced. When I show this writing to others, I get into trouble.

His chest and arms tingled as he picked up the phone. In those brief seconds his bladder pushed. He had to urinate. He was hoping it was Steve. In those brief seconds his resiliency resurged. The beginning tingling of horniness started in the tip and rippled through his groin.

"Hello."

The voice was female, perky, pushy, edged by refrained hysteria. It definitely was not Scott. He knew who it was. His bladder pushed harder. He had to urinate even more.

"Hey, how's it going? Guess what?"

"Hey. what's up? I don't know."

"I'm in town."

"You didn't move here, did you?"

"Are you crazy? I haven't had time yet to set that up. I have the weekend off. I just came to see you."

"Look, I don't mean to be rude, but you can't stay with me. Steve might come over. I have to keep things open for him."

"That's okay. I'm staying at the Kestlewick Inn. Besides Steve won't show up. I bet he's already made other plans. Like he always does. You know he doesn't love you. I'm the one who loves you."

"What a fucking bitch. You don't have to hurt me like that."

"Anyway, I have a great evening planned. We'll have dinner at L'Auberge. My treat. Then back to my room for some romance. I rented one of those love suites. you know, the ones with a heart-shaped water bed and a heart-shaped jacuzzi. Only this room is set up prehistoric-like—like your *Cave Painter* story. The one that pissed me off so much—almost as much as your *Getting High on the Bose-Einstein Condensate* one did. That was a load of crap. You know that, don't you? The bed has a genuine polar bear comforter, with the head and the pinkish clay tongue and the yellow teeth and everything. Oh, and the whirlpool is set in this bogus gray stone-you know the really cheap kind that you can tell is fake a mile away?-to resemble a cave. And so are the walls. I've ordered champagne and everything. It will be a blast."

"Unfuckingbelievable."

"So what time do you want me to come over and pick you up?"

"Look, Maggie, you've driven all this way to Iowa City from Chicago, and in some strange sense I suppose I should appreciate that. I guess I have to find time to see you. That would be the decent thing. But like I said, I have these plans with Steve. I"

"Fuck your plans with Steve. You don't turn him on. Nothing will ever happen between you. You're just a casual friend whom he fools around with now and then when he can't find anyone better. You stupid shit, wake up, your great love affair with Steve is only in your mind. Just as it's only in your mind that you are a fantastic writer—destined to be the greatest cultural figure of your generation—who so revolutionizes human thought that we become an advanced species. I've read the lastest trash you sent me. I have it right here in front of me. Let's see, how does it go? Oh yes. *I'm looking for Job. Will you help me find him in yourself? Actually I'm looking for Eve or Prometheus, but heroines and heroes are so hard to come by anymore.* But it is the same offensive crap as all your other work. You know, you're not even a good faggot. And you're an even worse writer."

"I'm supposed to listen to this?"

"Look baby, I'm sorry. It just makes me so angry when all I ever hear from you is Steve, Steve, Steve. What about me? I'm the one who loves you. I'm the one who will support you in your quest to become a great writer like myself. I can give you the world. What time should I pick you up, Honey? You know we'll have a good time. We always do."

"You always do."

"What about six? That will give me time to shower and get ready. I'll call and make reservations."

"Look, we can't set anything up—not until I find out what Steve is doing. Let me give him a call. I'll call you back. What's your number?"

"Yes, you do that. You call me back. Find out what time Steve is blowing you off, and then I'll pick you up at six."

"I have to go. I'll call you back."

"Oh, I forgot to bring protection. I left the stuff sitting out in the bathroom, but in my rush I"

"We're not having sex. Don't think that we're"

"Of course we're having sex. What's that line you always say: We did it so hard there was blood on the wall."

"I didn't say it; Sinead O'Connor did."

"We'll have dinner, and I'll be your dessert. And the sweat and the blood and the cum will mix into one hell of a cocktail."

"Are you on something?"

"No, baby, I just want to make love to you."

"We've been over this before. You know I'm gay."

"Yeah, yeah, you're gay—and you're the world's greatest writer—and Steve is madly in love with you."

"Do you want me to hang up?"

"The only reason you like men is because you've never had a woman like me."

"I have to go now."

"Wear something nice, but not too nice, because I'm going to rip it off you."

"I'll give you a call, but I mean it, don't get your hopes up."

Most evil is arbitrary. On close examination, much of the forbidden is merely imposition by people who say, "I don't have the flexibility or predisposition to like this, so I won't allow anyone else to like it either." But there is some evil that is definitely not this subjective. Murder might be one kind. Theft another. Depending upon the contexts and circumstances. And there is ostracism—being excluded from the group because the group cannot become large enough to welcome you. That seems like one of the biggest evils of all.

When I show my writings to people, I experience this evil firsthand.

Women have always been attracted to him. Jefferson thought as he put down the receiver and went to the bathroom to relieve himself. The tension from his bladder eased as did the tightness from that phone call. Especially fat, horny women who haven't had it in so many years that they are bloated with hormones. They would devour him in one episode.

But Maggie was neither fat nor horny. She was actually quite attractive. Admittedly her taste in fashion bordered on upscale Goodwill. But she had a slender body—kept trim from running, and running after men like Jefferson. Her waves of brown hair were not luxurious by any means, but they were striking in their heartiness and wholesomeness, somehow alluring; and they set off her perpetual dry mouth, with its accumulating rings of saliva that bordered her inner lips, and her high cheekbones, islands themselves surrounded by her once bright, now disappointed, brown eyes, and her sunken cheek bones emaciated by the hunger of loneliness. Her soft brown eyes were so full of pain, so full—like her voice—of imminent tears, so full of emptiness and waiting, but also so full of an overwhelming longing and sincerity and an undefeatable hope that they were quite inviting, relaxing. They lured him into the missed expectations of her life. He couldn't help but feel sorry for her. He couldn't help but do what he could to bring some happiness to her world, some sparkle to those eyes.

Finishing his duty and zipping himself up, he thought, it wasn't only women who found him attractive. Men found him handsome as well. And thank God for that , being the way he was. He knew what clothes to wear to stun the crowd when he went out to the bars. He knew what weights to lift, not only to keep his tall, sinewy body taut and suggestive, but to make his ass cheeks stand out firm and at attention. And he knew how to shake the product of his exercise on the rare occasions when it was late enough, and he was tired and drunk enough, to take the floor and dance.

He knew also that all the cute guys were watching. He knew what they were thinking and he knew that he would disappoint them. They would have to find someone else's brown hair to run their fingers through. As far as he was concerned, he was taken.

He even knew that Steve was watching him, though Steve always pretended not to. He was good at catching Steve in the act out of the corner of his eye, looking at Jefferson when Steve thought he wasn't looking. But when he got up the nerve to ask Steve what he was doing when the bar closed, his magical attraction lost its power.

Usually, Steve said, he was too tired. He just wanted to go home and sleep. Or he was just planning to watch TV and smoke pot with his friend Lance.

Sometimes, if Jefferson asked him in advance, his deflections would get more creative. "Would I like to do something this Friday? Okay. Oh wait, I have a concert. I'm sorry. And Saturday? I have a wedding. Maybe next weekend." And that excuse happened to be believable until Jefferson found himself driving past the concert hall, inadvertently, on that Friday night and was shocked to find the hall dark and peopleless, and he realized he had been lied to again.

The best excuses, though, were the ones Steve would use over and over again. Apparently he couldn't remember one story from the next. It must have been hard to keep track of them all. Like last week for instance. Jefferson asked him on Friday night if he was busy after the bar. Steve replied he had to go to the birthday party of a friend. She would be disappointed if he missed that. Jefferson said he understood. Then on Saturday night he asked Steve again. And again Steve was sorry. He had to go to the birthday party of a friend. She would be disappointed if he missed that. Jefferson said he understood, and he thought, "That must be one hell of a party— to last for two nights. That must be one hell of a woman—to have taken two days for her to have been born."

He just couldn't understand it. Everytime the eagerness of his eyes caught the same in Steve's blue ones he thought there was a connection, but it never happened. Maybe his eyes displayed that same pain and longing that Maggie's did. It would have been hard for them not to. Maybe that is what caught Steve's attention if only for a moment. Morning will erase surface despair but some of the resiliency will have been sapped. And it's been more than a few years since it has started to show. Maybe that display is what invited Steve so far in to the missed expectations of Jefferson's life that he couldn't help but feel sorry for him. Maybe that is what made him think that he would do what he could to bring some happiness to Jefferson's world, some sparkle to those eyes. And he would have. But, you see, he had this birthday party to attend.

shards–10,633

"She was what they called a pre-med. I never knew it mattered so much to her. All I know is that I missed her when she went away to the college. She had a full-ride scholarship at the fancy private university up in the capitol. Cute as a button, helped me harvest the corn every year since she was four years old. Sometimes she'd ride in the cockpit and talk to me. Other times she'd be waiting by the fence with my lunch and a thermos of iced tea."

A single, small tear blazed a trail down the dust of his cheek. He wiped it away before his two neighbors could notice. They sat staring at their coffee cups or the dried mud on their boots. Cars began to move past the implement store. Non-farmers on their way to work in the city.

Randall took a small gulp of coffee, swallowed hard, clearing his throat. His large, calloused hands warped the styrofoam container as he rested the dirt-creased cup on the striped lap of his overalls.

"They said it had something to do with something called nomenclature. Fancy names for chemicals. They said she missed other questions on the test regarding the workings of batteries. Bob told me she got a C on the test. It was her first one at the university. He said that C students don't get into medical school. Now Bob never finished college. He went one year at the state university to study agriculture. But books weren't for him. He came back to the farm. He said, 'Dad, I'm sorry I failed you, but this is where I belong.' I told him, 'Son, you didn't fail me. You found out something about yourself. That's worth more than all the degrees in the world.' His girl Katy was different than us. She was meant to be there. Always the star student. Smartest thing you ever saw. I didn't know learning about batteries had anything to do with studying to be a doctor."

A plane buzzed overhead. Sounds of orders and clanking of machines filtered in from the shop. A blonde haired man with a smile as bright as his youth put down the phone and confirmed to the men across the counter that their parts would be in by the end of the week. There would be no delay in the harvest.

Harvey shifted in his chair and scratched his forehead. Old Bill tapped slightly on his coffee. His cup was full and a few drops splashed out from his drumming. With a circular motion his boots polished the liquid into the concrete floor.

They had heard Randall's story before, all the details, three times--every fall, each anniversary since it happened. They listened attentively out of respect for their friend. It did not bore them.

"The doctors said she might have been saved, if she had been found in time. Her roommate didn't come back that evening. She had gone to a party and ended up going home with a boy she met there. They said Katy had done a good job with a knife. That's one thing a kid learns being raised on a farm. You see the answers were posted right after the test, so students could look on the wall and see how they did. Bob figures she must have seen the results, thought it was the end of the world, and gone right home to her dorm room to do it. Someone found her in the middle of the night. Another girl on her floor walking down the hall to use the restroom. The blood had flowed underneath the door from where she laid on the floor and stained the carpet in the hallway. I always thought she had such delicate wrists and hands. Pretty, you know. They cleaned the rug, but there was still a mark when we came to pick up her clothing and effects. It was pink and fanned out like a mushroom on the brown fibers. I stood facing it, touched the toes of my boots to its border. It looked like a flow—."

There was a break in his voice and a pause. He had long since learned to control his weeping, or at least to keep the ripples of convulsions inside, concealed to the outside world. No one knew about his walks to the barn, where he often collapsed to his knees, there among the hay and the cows, staring at him, silent. No one knew his most recent walk was just last month. With a fingernail he had pushed a crack into his cup. Coffee stained his pants leg.

Old Bill looked at Harvey. "It's good the crop's ready, Randall." His sight switched to Randall, slumped in his chair, then back to Harvey for confirmation of his verbal support. "It'll take your mind off it."

"That's what I keep thinking every year," Randall agreed, before draining the rest of his coffee down his throat. "I'll get busy with the farming and I'll forget what happened. All that hard work will be a tonic."

"I climb in that cab and look out over the golden rows, a sight that should make me think I am as rich as a king in ancient Sumeria. With the clear blue sky and the sun shining bright, the air apple crisp, what more could a man like me, a farmer, ask for in that time? Then I look at that seat next to me and I see how it is worn to the shape of the user and I see that it is empty, and I look toward the fence, and I don't make out anyone standing there with a wave and a brown paper sack and a silver thermos, and I know it's been three years and I know I got a job to do, and I turn the key and start the engine running and the noise scares up pheasants in front of me and I just don't have the heart in me. So I turn the combine off and I walk back to the house. Bob and Peg are waiting there on the porch, their arms around each other. They've added a lot of gray these last few years. Jeff, the hired hand, is standing behind them munching on a biscuit. I look at him and say, 'I'm sorry, Jeff, I guess you're on your own,' and Bob says, no, he'll spell him around ten. Jeff nods and starts walking toward the corn. I just go inside. I try not to look at anyone. Peg's hand brushes my shoulder as I pass her. Katy had a walkman. I sit down on the couch in the living room and put it on. I listen to the radio station. There is news, the farm reports, even some music. Not much of it interests me, but it keeps out the noise. I can't bear the sound, the sound of the combine whirring through the fields."

shards-165

The first questions posed of my dates, after the point we learned of HIV, used to be the obvious ones, the responsible ones—asked in ways, of course, more delicate than these: does the slit ever leak with a fluid that looks like snot? when you urinate does it feel like you must be passing acid? have there been any abrasions or pimples on your genitalia that I should know about? Have you had the test for AIDS? When was the last time? What were the results? On those infrequent times when you lie on your stomach and endure the pain disguised as pleasure, do you use a condom?

But then my questions became more sophisticated: Read this quote by the Planck Institute physicist Bernd-Olaf Küppers: "This means: the origin of biological information can indeed be explained as a general phenomenon, but the concrete content of biological information cannot be deduced from the laws of chemistry and physics."[1] What does that mean to you? Explain to me the wisdom contained in Danah Zohar's *The Quantum Self* and Charles Taylor's *The Ethics of Authenticity;* wisdom of the complex, fluid, engaged, celebrant interaction of human minds the authors can't help but express but don't even know themselves. (Prescience, it is called.) What does it mean to be starcarbon twinkling as language, culture, affection, interpretation? Can you see yourself as light— both wave and particle? More importantly, can you overlap that energy with the photons of others? Can you see yourself as shadow? If I read you this poem fragment by Rainer Maria Rilke: "...and leave you, (inexpressibly to unravel)/ your life, with its immensity and fear,/ so that, now bounded, now immeasurable,/ it is alternately stone in you and star"[2]—what would be a meaning you would ascribe to it? At the end of my questioning, before you put your arms anywhere close to me, before your tongue turned my mouth into a chalice and sipped the wine of my spit, could you see that everything we talked about was wrapped in the petaled ending of this Louise Glück lilies poem: "then white light/ no longer disguised as matter."[3] Would that phrase become your Golden Rule? An absolute and only commandment?

None of those questions matter anymore. Forgive the absence of tact. I get right to the point. I know our blood pressure is rising. I can feel our skin sparkling with electricity. Your pants are being reshaped according to your hardness. And I want to mess around with you as much as you do with me. There's just one thing I have to know. Have you ever thought seriously about killing yourself? Can you describe for me the grainy, almost bitter, texture of the first of many sleeping pills dissolving in your mouth, as you press a glass of water to your lips to wash them down? Has your saliva ever watered to the scent of steel while your jaws twitched in an unfamiliar way; your tongue caressing a metal barrel cutting hard into your upper palate? When was the last time you felt the palms of your hands go white against the cold and clammy railing of a bridge; the whirling water below churning a lorelei enchantment, calling you to a restful euphoria? You know what I mean?—the times you're driving home for Christmas and the interstate is slick with ice and danger and the visibility is so poor that all you can see are four of the eighteen wheeler's tires in front of you; a cushion you could slide into, speeding up and out of control, so the burden of the cargo comes crushing down upon you, and there's nothing left except shards of glass painted with the tempera of your skin that some boyscout on a roadside clean-up detail finds the next spring. Please don't be offended. It's not that I don't trust you. There are just things in this day and age we need to negotiate before sex. I was just wondering.

Have you ever thought about these things?

If the answer is no, I spring from the futon of his quaint, but queer, enclave, break from the embrace, and walk away. Say good-bye only out of politeness.

He remains in the dark, trembling, his heart pounding to the beat of my fading footsteps. He is deflating with each thud of the heart, a retraction, like the erratic lowering of a crane; a withdrawal from glory, disappearing into the unassuming presence of its ordinary softness. Not much different than an adored superstar who can glitter on stage and dazzle, mesmerizing the audience, but afterwards must huddle in the cave of his dressing room, words spoken only in a whisper, letting the answering machine respond to the phone, keeping perfectly quiet at each knock of the door.

shards-134

...and I would write a book about you, an elegy that would make the generations to follow weep, had I the talent.

shards-133

So I didn't send you flowers, "with everything else, and you: we fin-
ish, wipe off the bodily fluids, zip up, and go out together into the
night: it's New Year's Eve and the night is,"[4] though I could understand why David would want to. He, like I, when he spent the
night with you, fell asleep in the arms of a god. In his book *My Own
Country* my friend and teacher Abe Verghese writes, "Rajani
believes that safety can be found in the old conventions. But I have
come to believe that human life is fast and fleeting and that our
moments of safety are rare."[5] With you, that night, I had these
moments, and peace, even joy. And when I rose and closed the door
to your room; your eyes following me there, then to the window as
I exited your house—the splendid taste of memory on my tongue,
filtering into my nose—and headed for my car, I walked into the

sun of an unremarkable morning. My exhilaration numbed by an aging body aching for some sleep.

I'm too old for this, I thought: these games. And yet what else, but this hope these games turn into permanence, is there to live for? My mind racing around inside my head ran into the soft cotton dullness of fatigue. Oh, to be able to go to bed, this time to sleep, but I was heading home to start a busy and brand new day: Arising to a dawn filled with thoughts of you that made me feel like the sun was setting all over again, at seven o'clock in the morning, and we were heading into the landscape of a Stephen Beachy night: "so excellent, bound to disappoint, but still: we can go anywhere in it, anywhere at all." [4] So that from your house to mine, driving along the streets, not once did I have to stop, not once did I slow down, all the way home, each light turning green as I approached it.

shards-128

I want Morten Harket to make love to me with *Memorial Beach* playing in the background, especially the songs, *Dark Is the Night for All* and *Cold As Stone.* He stands on the cover of the album in white pants, a black belt, and matching leather jacket, with his hair slicked back and his right knee slightly bent, almost contrapasto, beckoning. Then on the back photo of the jewel CD case his overture becomes more explicit. His jacket has been removed and hangs down opposite that still bent knee; his right arm resting on that thigh before curving up the S to his turned, bare shoulder. This image captured a second before he circles it in the air, a wave to Come along. And those eyes, they give no doubt—in the centerfold of the lyrics book—peering out from behind a pole, like the lone alpha male standing in the snow of a Jim Brandenburg photo. His stare draws you in, to his ripe lips, a dinner, then all the way deep, past those seeing stars. The face is black-and-white but surely those eyes are Caprian blue, or maybe a mysterious green, tinted with gray, dusted with a shadow of purple, and you float into another universe where the climax is your mind exploding; expanding into a joy you have yet not known.

What's so unreasonable about that? Is that too much to ask? Well? Is it?

Dark is the night for all. Not if you're lying next to him. His dried cum crackling the hairs on your chest. Your mouth still dancing—there, a few drops on your tongue, tingling.

shards—2,172

This was a very unusual request—the funeral director, Percival, adorned in stylish Pierre Cardin gold-framed glasses and the best gray suit and black patent leather wingtips that Sears had to offer, whispered to her, his face all bunched constipation-like. Quite odd, he added, shaking his head and losing the grace of his professional demeanor. And before all these people, meaning those gathered for the funeral, it just didn't seem appropriate.

Heather, who was at the beginning of a career where she would work her way successfully from first admission into one of the nation's most prestigious dental schools, then into one of the most competitive oral surgery residencies, before coming to head one of Chicago's most reputable and profitable oral surgery practices, knew something about asserting herself and was not about to be daunted over a matter as important to her as this by a man who dressed himself and asserted himself as poorly as he did. She agreed her timing could have been better, but this would be her last chance, the casket about to be closed forever.

Their conversation was muted to the general, seated onlookers in the pews by the haunting strains of U2's *Love is Blindness,* which made their animated, though restrained, discussion seem a distorted pantomime.

> *Love is clockworks*
>
> *And cold steel*
>
> *Fingers too numb to feel*
>
> *Squeeze the handle*
>
> *Blow out the candle*
>
> *Love is blindness[6]*

And the church was full of them. The onlookers, that is. If Jim— or James or Jimmy to his red-eyed, tear-stained cheeks parents and siblings sitting in the front row—had known that so many people had cared for him, so many people admired him—at least they told themselves—it would have made a difference.

At least he told himself, it would have made a difference, if they had taken more pain, more conscientiousness, more explicitness, to show it-while he was alive.

> *A little death*
>
> *Without mourning*
>
> *No call*

And no warning

Baby...a dangerous idea

That almost makes sense[6]

It could have made a difference. But he knew otherwise. There was only one who mattered.

I hate to place all the burden on you, Edward, he told him in an imaginary conversation. My life was a mess before I met you...and it is still a mess. You are the only one I've ever found who could change it. You are the only one who can save me.

"I just want you to know," Edward replied, in a real conversation, "that I've told the police about this. I don't appreciate your threatening phone calls or your freakish letters. They're sick. You've got to move on I tell you."

This was Edward's morality of one. The world, especially the people in it, especially the people that he used now and again for comfort, had to conform wholly to Edward's rules, conform to his needs. Maybe that was his philosophy, it dawned on Jim. Maybe Edward just used people until he wore out his welcome, fearing, or not capable of, getting more than superficial with anyone, and then just moved on. Maybe that was as sincere as Edward could get— offering this dysfunctional philosophy of his to others.

But move on Jim could not. He was stuck with Edward-in a downward spiral of destruction, that perhaps started at birth, though it definitely was in full swirl, dragging him into the quick-sand, as a young boy, a young man, as a man up until his at age 25 demise, when he realized, laying in bed at night, feeling a tingle in his groin that made him smile, that warmed him, comforted him, took away his loneliness, a sensation brought on by the thought of

lying in the grasp of another man, until that thought became the
only one that could drag him out of bed in the morning, after he
had relieved that thought into his hands and his bedsheets, that
would now need to be laundered, until that thought and its relief,
could not even drag him out of bed, until that thought could not
even stimulate him, and he would just want to lay there in bed, the
sun rising, his room getting warmer, and the phone ringing, his
compatriots at work calling, worried, wondering why he hadn't
shown up for his shift, but there was no answer, even though the
phone was right beside the bed, in arm's length, yet he could not
move, and he wouldn't have been able to speak had he been able
to pick up the receiver.

This eddy of downward spiral had him locked tight in its tor-
nado. So when Edward told him "move on, I cannot help you, I
don't care," he grasped at Edward's ankles, standing on the solid
ground before him, trying to pull him in, trying to take Edward
with him, but the wet sand made it hard to hold on to Edward's
black Ked's high tops, and he lost his grip. He wanted Edward to
come along but he was sucked into the ground, alone, disappearing
into a darkened, moist pressure that collapsed his lungs and mind,
and actually felt good after all he had lived and just gone through.

The hole closed up and around him, leaving only a wet spot, a
target upon which Edward urinated before he turned and walked
away—grinning inwardly at his masterful control of his manipula-
tory talents; skills that had been so severely and persistently chal-
lenged by this insignificant player. Edward felt more 100% right of
himself in his morality-of-one than ever.

The crowd continued to look on in curious and mounting dismay
as Heather insisted her point, pulling a blue and red plaid woolen
blanket from a Nordstrom's bag, with a tranquil Grant Wood
painting reproduced on its sides. Percival, the funeral director,

more uncomfortable in his name and more bunched up like a shriv-
elled anus than ever, his hemorrhoids starting to seep a trickle of
blood, looked desperately over to the family, especially to the parents (who these last few days seemed to have travelled ten years farther down the road from stoutness to frailty) for support, but found
only, at best, disinterest. Perhaps he even saw their approval and
gratitude in Heather's actions. Afterall, she was a friend of their
tormented (a recent discovery) son, trying to say good-bye in a truly
touching and personal way. So Percival acquiesced to them and
conceded to her, deciding that the best way to get rid of her specta-
cle was to let her go about it and get it over with. He did admonish
her to be quick and nonchalant about it.

Appalled, yet obedient to her request, he lifted the lower lid of the
casket, which concealed the pelvis and legs of the deceased, while
she unfolded the blanket. Percival was sweating, nervously by now,
his armpits starting to add moisture to previous rings of accumu-
lated stains, and he dared not make eye contact with the now wholly
attentive and at once quiet audience. Heather, not to make the
director any more uncomfortable than he was, quickly covered
those exposed legs and pelvis. He stood to the side, of no help what-
soever, and nearly fainted. She tucked her friend in, just as she
would her own children a few years later, by herself pulling the
blanket up and under his folded arms to his neck, so that its wooly
consistency might scratch him comfortably underground. She had
to lift his hands to do this. They were deadweight and she did not
weigh more than 120 pounds. But it was 120 pounds of determination. She struggled lifting the limbs' stiffness and heaviness up and
folding them back down on top of the blanket. This finished, Percival, concealing a nervous fart, that sounded in the room anyway,
quickly and firmly snapped down the bottom half of the lid of the

casket, wiped his sweaty palms on the sides of his suit jacket, and briskly disappeared into an anteroom to compose himself.

Alone now, placing her shopping bag on the floor, resting it against the knee-pad railing on the bottom of the casket gurney, Heather reached over and placed an elegant-looking roll-call of names—laser-printed on expensive, buff-colored resume paper— on the lavender interior satin of one side of the coffin.

She whispered in his ear, "I brought you a blanket." Laughing softly at a private joke. "I hear it's cold where you are going." And even if you are going nowhere, she thought, biting back her lip, biting back a tear that fell anyway, followed by several more, "at least you'll be warm."

She knew he smiled back in gratitude-if that was possible. He was that kind of guy.

> *Love is drowning.*
>
> *In a deep well*
>
> *All the secrets*
>
> *And no one to tell*
>
> *Take the money*
>
> *Honey*
>
> *Blindness*[6]

Motioning with her eyes, she called attention to the slip of paper. "It's the roll call of friends you gave me." This was a list, he once showed her, that contained all the names, over his twenty-five years, of people he wanted to have as friends, of people who could not give as much of themselves to others as he was willing to give

to them. "Their memory will go with you. Someday they will realize what a loss they suffered."

"No they won't," he would have said. "But thank you for your
kind lie. The thought can almost make it real."

She anticipated his next question, "No, he didn't come. I haven't
seen him anyway. I think he needs some time. He's taking this
pretty hard. Really. He is. He did care, very much, even though he
pretended not to. You know as well as I that was his defense mech-
anism. One day I'm sure he'll visit you. One day I'm sure he'll
think of you."

Again, he would have said, thank you for your lies.

> *Love is blindness*
>
> *I don't want to see*
>
> *Won't you wrap the night*
>
> *Around me*
>
> *Take my heart*
>
> *Love is blindness*[6]

Her last act, she bent down, kissing him on the forehead, gently
stroking, once, the fine tuft of his fine brown hair. "Remember that
dream you told me? You were riding in a car with Edward, play-
fully slapping one another, driving who knows where, but driving
as best of friends, he pretending to be annoyed (by your letters and
phone calls of crying out for his attention), but he could not hide his
smile, that wonderful, magnificent, one million watt smile, he could
not hide his happiness? Remember how you told me that was the
best dream you ever had? Keep that dream in your thoughts. Take

it into your sleep. If it's all you have, if it's all you've ever wanted, then take it with you. Move on, but take it with you."

Years later, walking down Michigan Avenue, sometimes, shopping, a bulging Nordstrom's bag in one hand, an equally overflowing Saks in the other, she gets so cold that she runs, awkwardly, in heels, to her apartment on Oak Street, above the Armani boutique, and turns up the heat, to 80 degrees. In the sweltering, sizzling, dripping August day, her houseguests and family complain, sweat, and beg for air conditioning. Still she cannot warm herself.

She tears through closets and drawers, rooms one by one, throwing their contents on the floor, half frightening her children, looking for that red and blue plaid woolen blanket, a family heirloom gift from her grandmother, so many years ago when she was a girl. Frantic, not able to find it, almost ready to scream out. Then stopping short, gasping, breath frozen, sucked only half way down the throat, she touches her clavicle, on the left side with her right hand, sheds a tear, cracks a half smile, and remembers.

Wright, her partner, startled by her unannounced approach from behind, sitting in a leather chair in his den, planning his next ski trip, as soon as decent powder in Colorado warrants it, the insidious Amendment 2 an insidious memory repealed many years ago, is equally surprised by her full force bear hug around his neck and her assertion at how lucky she is. How extremely lucky she is.

And still, sometimes, she cannot warm herself.

shards-832

The drab grey flannel and navy blue world of my corporate accounting office makes a perfect backdrop for the conversation piece sculpture I have on my desk. It is a commission of a space shuttle orbiting an apple. When my clients ask me for an explanation, nothing more adequate seems forthcoming than the fact that it reminds me of some dear people I knew long ago. I do not tell them as I frequently adjust my tie—something noticeable to new clients as a nervous tic, a sight regular clients do not even process— that I am fingering, in reality, a necklace of three rings and a locket underneath my shirt. One ring belongs with my wife, our wedding band. The other two rings are those of my parents, my second pair, the two elderly men who unofficially adopted me and saved my life. The locket contains a picture of Jenny Holm, a neighborhood girl from my childhood. Jenny was quote unquote the girlfriend of my sixth grade brother. The fact that I, and not my brother, have possession of this locket today is how this story all got started in the first place.

The accounting life has been good to me. A full partner in an international firm, my CPA salary has afforded me some of life's material acoutrements, including a country spread, just fifty miles to the north of Chicago. A rustic house, an equally quaint and weathered barn, and a small acreage dotted with fruit trees. I grew up with a small orchard of apple, pear, and peach trees in our suburban back yard, so it reminds me of home, if one wants to be reminded of such: those happy times, hanging out with my older brother, back when I still could believe, unconditionally, that the world was good and there was no reason to question it.

When talking about how I acquired this work of art, I do not tell my clients how often I churn wakeless at night. My thoughts rouse me from my bed. My wife mumurs contently, her empty arms' grasps my pillow and air. I walk outside to the orchard and ponder past moments of my life that I just cannot make go away, times I just cannot ever bring back.

I do this periodicially even through autumn, sitting out there sometimes in nothing more than a flannel bathrobe and open-heeled slippers. The air does not chill me. I have placed a park bench in a spot clear from trees. The aroma of apples and the futile, yet hopeful, song of a stubborn cricket sooth me. I sit there on that bench, all alone, and look into the sky. The nights where the heavens are clear and the stars shine down-those are my favorite.

I let my clients reach their own conclusions about my sculpture. (It never fails to elicit a remark from them.) After all, doesn't the interpretation and value of art lie in the eyes and mind of the beholder?

I certainly do not tell them about the necklace. They wouldn't understand. The sculpture is only a fragment of the tale, anyway, an afterthought, a historical chronicling. I do not tell them the whole story. I barely tell them the beginning-only that it reminds of me of my family, my brother and my parents. This is enough. It seems to satisfy them. They would not be prepared for what I would tell them if I told them everything. And I would not want to have to pick them up off the floor once they've fallen off their chairs, having made a mess of themselves.

It is so tranquil and reassuring sitting underneath the trees and peering up at the dark. Though I must admit, lately, this activity has become an obsession for me. It's happening almost every night. My wife has suggested psychiatric help. A prescription for Valium will, I think, do for now. I remain there usually for an hour, once in awhile two. Sometimes a harsh mist will slap against my face, or a fierce wind will whip leaves through the branches and tangle them in my hair. Often, when the onset of dew or frost blankets my inert mass as well, I cannot be distinguished from the grass. I fell asleep once out there. My wife, frantic, found me on the bench with my clothes as white as the ground. Our golden retriever returned color to the fabric of my clothes with the warm pulses of her breath.

Maybe what puts me out there is that I am looking for a sign; a shooting star, a newtonian apple plunking my head, the trail of a shuttle's vapor billowing white against the midnight. Greetings from someone in my past—a dear brother cupping a wave like a homecoming queen to let me know he is okay. Though these signals never come, I usually persist until I see the light of a far-off jet moving UFO-like across the sky. A symbolic victory. Or at least I hold out for the red lights of a locally-piloted Cessna blinking its way above the fields adjacent to my farm. When this happens I always wave-a full-armed wave, palms open and fingers extended, both arms wiper-washing the night.

Though it is dark and the occupants of the aircraft are too distant to see my commotion, it is not really to them that I signal. I wave until exhaustion and foolishness overtakes me. I wave until the lights disappear from the strength of my vision. A slight film of sweat covers my forehead, but not before I have already turned away and am heading back towards the house. I wave but I do not look. I do not want to know if my greeting ever gets returned. Or if it doesn't.

shards–1341

And you turn to him, smile, kiss him again and again before you ask, without a thought of guilt, what was your name again. It's too early for him to protest your lapse of memory, and he's too sweet to care, or too tired to notice; and a whisper purses through his lips and forms the name Joseph. and your soul sinks back on the bed in contentment. and you smile. It was not a dream. It is real. And as your body leaves heading for the door you brush a hand across his cheek just to make sure. And his brown eyes pool in kindness and look up at you, a glint of longing streaking across their surface. And the cheek is soft and smooth. And it presses warmly against the back of your fingers—a contact that is only fractional—but you do your best to hold onto it forever.

shards—6,590

Look at these hands! How they paw the pages of this book and bend them back. Brutes! Steady, now, steady. Hold firmly with all your might. Don't let the tremors be evident. Fingers, give support to my voice to keep it from cracking. Oh palms, cup around my lips, give resonance to what comes out, let my mouth do what it was asked to do.

One by one we circled the table. Each person gave their name and a reason for being here. All eyes upon me now. I felt the stares warm the callused and scarred fists that opened the book to the permanent break in the spine on page thirty-four. "This what I want to do. I want to write a poem like this." Then my hands held tight and I began reading these lines as if they were my own.

You are not beautiful, exactly.

You are beautiful, inexactly.

You let a weed grow by the mulberry

and a mulberry grow by the house.

So close, in the personal quiet

of a windy night, it brushes the wall

and sweeps away the day till we sleep.

A child said it, and it seemed true:

"Things that are lost are all equal."

But it isn't true. If I lost you,

the air wouldn't move, nor the tree grow.

Someone would pull the weed, my flower.

The quiet wouldn't be yours. If I lost you,

I'd have to ask the grass to let me sleep[7].

A woman gasped as I finished. I pushed the book towards the circle, open, there. There, this is my reason. My poetry teacher nodded his head. "A noble task," he said.

My tongue was dry. These last few days, I think I cried out all the tears inside me. Licking the envelope, sealing it shut, seemed like the final end to our relationship. The poem was inside, finished. There was one more task, one more saying good-bye, and that was to deliver it to him.

The roads to his apartment complex seemed part of some mystical world where there was no sound, or at least where I lost the ability to hear it. The rush of cars on all sides of me had been muted by someone's remote control. Music blared from each speaker of the stereo but none of the notes reached me. When my car turned into the parking lot and came to rest three stalls from his front door, the entire world had stopped what it was doing, pulled up a chair to listen to this poem, my supposed masterpiece.

I didn't even knock. There was ample space to catch the paper in a crack between the door and the jam, right above the golden-colored knob. That's where I shoved it in. I did not know whether he was home or not. It didn't matter. Someone would find it next time the entrance was opened. A slight breeze caught hold of it as I walked back to my car. The envelope wagged briefly in the wind as I drove away watching it in my rearview mirror. A final wave goodbye?

At home I brewed some tea, turned on the Sox game, twirled the pen that had written the poem in these, my, hands. When he ripped the envelope open to read my last greeting would he be thinking my own thoughts: "Is this the best you can do? Didn't I lead you to any greater inspiration?" I never claimed to be Marvin Bell.

These hands rubbed themselves together as I waited across town for his review, as if I were a young writer pacing a path on the porch of a workshop colleague while she sat inside reading my latest work, doing all that I could to keep from rushing in at any minute to yell, "So what do you think?" What pathetic old paws I had. How many women did they support myself above in my younger days. How they caressed the mother of my children with struggling tenderness, against the grain of their natural roughness. They held a son and a daughter above my head, felt the giggles of their glee at this game as I whooshed them to the ceiling. Count the burns and scrapes and cuts they suffered tending molten iron at the forge. Measure the force of their fingers, of myself, pressing into him in what came to be my second life. Smooth hand lotion into their wrinkles of age and insanity that gave them the ego to write this poem:

I wish I could call all the stars out
to dance just for you[8]

To order the heavens
I cannot do.
What use to wish
that Hallmark sentiment
had such power.
Close the card

on this concern. Marvel
at the black sky, twinkling—
whatever is responsible for it—and realize
this whole wonderful dark mess
up there is my wish
for you, completed already.

His hands put the folded sheet down. They are free of blemish, protected by the gloves of youth. I cannot see if he smiles. I assumes that he does. His approval. Then he puts the poem away into a box of cherished memories. And we are done.

My days of poetry are also past. Well, I'll continue to read poetry. I mean, I don't see the need to write it. These hands have tried to soften the hardness of everything they have grasped. They will move on to something else. But if, in a lyrical moment, they ever chance to pick up a pen again and put beauty down on paper, I'd like to add one more stanza and send it to him.

> *Look at these hands! These ugly, clumsy clubs.*
>
> *See what dribble they write?*
>
> *Who or what could they possibly move?*
>
> *They're not much. They're all I have.*
>
> *Remember this. They're all I have.*
>
> *With them.*
>
> *Any time.*
>
> *I will cradle you.*

whole

With that I was finished and I turned to him to sense his contentment, my hands covering my eyes to the glow of his adoration. "That's quite an imagination you have," he would say. "Sad, maybe sick, but fantastic. Where do you come up with all these things?" And I would beam and say, "I can imagine anything in the world." Then add softly, "except happiness." Then add, just in my thoughts, except being with someone for more than three weeks. "Is any of it true?" he would question. I would turn to grab him with assurance that yes, indeed, much of what I've said is true, at least in a way.

My lips stop moving and my words float into our memories, and he's still here, and all this did not scare him away. So I reach out to hold onto him but my arms flop through dead space and land on the spot that he vacated hours ago in my autobiography. The indentation of his presence has remolded to the flatness of the mattress. My fingers sense the coldness of the sheet, his warmth long gone, dissipated into the anonymity of the larger world.

My torso swings around to check the rest of the room. I feel glass against my hand, hear glass clinking against its own, watch a goblet tumble from the nightstand, rolling over itself in slow motion, out into the air, a few droplets of wine spraying bloodlike, dramatically, as if from a wound. My hand grasps at its spiral, a one-handed acrobatic catch of the winning, come-from-behind touchdown in the endzone. Its fall is broken and it does not shatter into a zillion pieces. Still, it is injured. There is a guttural cry like the death moan of a gazelle caught in the jaws of a lion. Or is it the sound of a crack, a split in the smooth fluid seam of the goblet? My fingers grasp the stem at the end of its trajectory to soften the bounce at the floor. I have prevented total disaster—if one can call saving an artist's life whose hands have been cut off in a horrible accident a rescue. The heirloom I hold is almost intact but irreparably dysfunctional. An opaque line of dissent framing a small hole of escape. The bowl of the antique crystal can hold liquid no more, and as I cuddle the ruined treasure in my hand there is not a void large enough to contain my silence.

The disapproving eyes of my great-grandfather look down upon me. I am sorry we had to meet under these circumstances. His cast is more of forlorn than anger. And I cannot think of a glue, any method of repair, that can make his handiwork whole again. Like new.

Though, like my fantastic tales, I can conjure him up in my imagination, I cannot pull his workshop out of the air. The hot coals, the glass glowing red like neon, the metal pinchers holding the molten sand as he shapes the clear and hardening liquid into beauty. A piece of art so fragile, yet so enduring, that I can pour the liquid of grapes into it over a hundred years later and toast the pleasantries of life with a friend. Except now it is flawed, incurably diseased, and whatever is offered into it now will leak out like a slow agonizing death.

There is no mistake. This is not a dream. Rays of dawn begin to light up the room, burning the mist of sleep off my eyes. The crack feels rough under my thumb. It is sharp, capable of cutting a line in my skin. Though I have imagined many things this night, this tragedy is not one of them. The defect is there, a treasure is ruined, and I am the only one sitting up in my bed.

Whatever stories of my life I have fantasized and actually experienced in the realities of others, last night's myth is not one of them. Did last night even happen? Whoever that man was, whatever his name, he must have been a product of rapid eye movement. Something that comes in the gray ambiguity of night. Even if he did exist, what does it matter?: he isn't here now. He won't be here in three weeks. Whatever we thought we had, it didn't last the night.

I put my feet on the floor and walk across to the window and peer out at the sun. Every day it continues its rise, this morning included, and takes me along for the ride, whether I like it or not. I rest the goblet on the chipped paint of the window sill, pondering whether it is worth keeping. How would I explain it to future guests? "It used to be of value?" With a shrug of the shoulders? "Now it is worthless." Like it didn't matter? The pair it came from were my only wine glasses. In the future do I offer libations in the other intact one and in a "matching" red plastic cup?

I'm guessing that he left right at sunrise for the kaleidoscope was also sitting on the ledge. It had been moved from its display space on a bookshelf. I had bought a new one three months ago as a present when I got my first job out of college and moved to my new city. Perhaps he took me up on my suggestion to look at the patterns using the source from the first light of day.

Watching the shards of color sequentially build into a crescendo of a multicolored palette becoming brighter and brighter like the rose window at Notre Dame, professionally lit for the photographer of the postcards that are hawked all over Paris, is a great way to start one's morning.

At any rate, that is where the kaleidoscope was, and I do not see how it could have gotten there in any other way. The note scratched on a piece of paper left underneath it was the most convincing evidence of all. It said, "Thanks for a wonderful evening. I had to go in a rush, a boyfriend thing, but I kissed you good-bye. Give me a call sometime. Give me a call SOON!" Underneath his printed first name, Adrian, he had written his phone number: 341-8407.

At least that's what I remembered. At least that's what I made up. The wind from the night before had not subsided and a grasp of it pulled the note from my loose hold and sent it fluttering down the street, a maple leaf falling a month early. I cannot prove any of this incident to any one. No longer can I prove any of it to myself.

In the distance I caught a shadow walking away from my house. He was blocks away. Or she was. I couldn't determine a gender, nor even the color of this person's shirt. But I was pretty sure it was him. I put the wooden tube to my eye, as if I held instead a telescope, and tried to bring him in focus. The refraction of light this individual created did not even register any distinction in the prism. The color did not get any brighter. But then it also did not dilute one photon.

I put the kaleidoscope down. Was this a memorable evening? What had happened in between the daze of my babbling, our encounter, and my obvious dozing that allowed him to disappear unnoticed?

A spark caught my eye. The sun had aimed its beam at the slit in the broken wine glass and intensified a ball of light shining into my room like a spotlight. The glass seemed on fire and trembled, ready to explode or come to life.

I focused the sight of the kaleidoscope on this blazing ball of light. It burned a round spectral glare in the center of the fragmented design. The color within its penny-sized circumference was brilliance magnified as brilliance. It became three-dimensional and danced like a rotating sphere. I saw his face smiling back at me. I saw us together on dates, at home cooking dinner after long days at work, in bed drinking wine. There was a permanence in the luminosity of the light, a promise that said this relationship would not fade.

I do not know anymore what I imagine, and what I experience. There are those whose say the former will determine the latter. I cannot say for certain that this small star in the center of my kaleidoscope was moving. There is only one thing now of which I am certain. That light within the light of my kaleidoscope was real as the round tube of wood I held in my hand. I am unable to say what this event means in the course of my life, but whenever I look at the reflection of hope that rose into dawn through the wound of the glass, focusing it on the chaotic canvas of my own life, whenever I look into the brilliance upon the brilliance, the spot I see is shimmering. Bright and loud and shimmering.

The world of my bedroom becomes a Matta painting *Like Me, Like X*. Its canvas an explosion of glass shards, with one blue eye watching the expansion. One blue eye of mine is in the lower left hand corner of the painting, right in the path of the splintering glass and fury exploding out into the world. Behind this activity I cannot make out anything whole. The colors are hot and cold, blue and red, and I see torsos intertwined, twisted. Limbs grasping, radiating light, pulling others close, into something more. Into me.

Should the sun change position in the sky, rising higher in the day, and the leaves of a tree in front of this house block forever this once-in-a-lifetime view, I will know what this was that was forming as it left me. What is still forming inside of me, not yet finished, pulling itself into something more complete.

From the outside, if he pauses four blocks away, turns and looks back to remember, the scene on the second story must look to him like a pastel of Odilon Redon; an iconoclastic girl with bouquet looking longingly out of one of two arched stone windows. Only what he sees is not a *Mystical Painting of Girl and Flowers*. I am a boy and kaleidoscope, moving my fingers in fits and scratches across the narrow catching, searching for any conceivable position to allow that crystal to recapture the glowing spot.

There are two windows in this view. One is empty and blue—sad and waiting for him, for others. How fitting the blue shade is for my loneliness. The other frames the fullness of me. My face is illuminated but not by the sun. Solar beams glint upon the dust of the windowsill. Orange flickers encased in gold leaf spark up at me, brightening my face, as if this is the very moment of hope and this instant is fire on a string. The expression I have could be the memory of last night with him or the anticipation of such an evening in the near future. I'd like to leave this open to both interpretations.

No one would mistake me for an artist. This does not prevent me from cradling a cool piece of charcoal among my fingers and thumb, rubbing this real image out of the rough black paper, to have a painting like this for my very own. I draw the meshing of torsos and the crossing of limbs from nothing but this blank sheet and a box of colors. This work may command my occasional attention over a long period of time—just to get it right. To make it complete. If I ever do.

No one has to tell me this work of art can do little but offer therapy and comfort. It cannot bring him, or anyone, back into my tangible space. But if it never becomes powerful enough to transcend its two-dimensional existence and warp itself into living flesh, to seal my unfixable break and become my present reality, then I will think of this poem,

> *Kiss me*
> *On the lips*
> *On the eyes*
> *Our name will be forgotten*
> *In time*
> *No one will remember our work*
> *Our life will pass*
> *like the traces of a cloud*
> *And be scattered like*
> *Mist that is chased by the*
> *Rays of the sun*
> *For our time is the passing*
> *of a shadow*
> *And our lives will run like*
> *Sparks through the stubble*[9]

and my painting of sparks, hanging on a wall, will always serve to remind: this, him, once whole, we. This has been made my history.

I must add one small, final thing to this event. The brooding vacant window next to me resonates still with the blue and vibrations of his shadow. Another's presence, once touched, cannot ever fully leave you. Those gilded sparks in front of me are jumping over to that void, faint yet determined, so far from their source. They swirl vaguely up into something of substance. In this image I can almost make out a figure. I am beginning to see the glow behind his eyes. I blink, the lenses in my head re-crystallize, become molten, blow themselves into something capable of holding wine—or of bringing his face back into focus. My fingers reach out, and who they touch is no longer imagination.

Afterword

For Ric Graf and Tess Catalano,

and for all those who came before, the ones we've forgotten, the ones we still hold dear, and the ones we never got to meet.

For David Goodwin,

*dreams can come true
victories can be achieved.*

For Mathew Shepard and Brandon Tina,

you are loved and cradled in our thoughts.

Life is short, walk slowly.

Tess Catalano

About the Author

Copernicus again is founding director of the Iowa International Center for Queer (Fluid) and Complex Lives, informally known as the House of Wonder—the Learning Center for Joy and for *your* Human Possibility. He claims no other identity than this: "Hello, my name is Adrian, a being celebrantly open to my human possibilities." He hopes all others will abandon their binary mythologies and monolithic lives and use their imagination and courage to expand into their paradoxical—simply complex, stably fluid— and sophisticated, or Adrianic, identities.

Copernicus again wanders the world looking for his twelve husbands and his twelve wives. Along the way he is content to do his part to create a new mythology for the new human species, *Homo adrians;* one finally ready to celebrate and embrace its stable fluidity and simple complexity. He writes and collects the literature that will be definition of the new human species. He commissions and collects the art that will become the new species' image.

He declares, "Let there be light and darkness. In the beginning was the word and the image. And it was good and bad and paradoxical and real, gloriously.

Copernicus again is author of the forthcoming books on truth *(Burst)*, sexuality *(Humansexuality)*, moral love *(The Sex closest* to "God": *Why same-sex affection is the most moral human inti-macy),* and identity rights *(How to win the Nobel Prize: The Ulti-mate push to achieve unequivocal ad irrevocable rights for those who find joy in same-sex affection.)* He is also the prophet and author of *GALAP* –Guidelines for an Authentic Life in the Age of Paradox–which is a necessary replacement of the Ten Command-ments as a fundamental moral tenet.

I will leap into my grave with joy knowing I was responsible for infecting the dominant fear discourses of rigidity, simplicity, binary and monolithism with an ultimately, if not rapidly, fatal virus. From this plague a new renaissance will emerge, and discourses of joy—fluidity, complexity, paradox, and multiplicity—will allow individuals and cultures to be congruent, finally, with true and jubilant human possibility.

Copernicus again

Appendix

Commentary on Fracture and the writings of Copernicus again

I look forward to reading Copernicus again's works as it is always a pleasure. I must admit, that at first, the boldness of his approach indeed shocked me. Yet, he administers these shocks without pulling punches or flinching, and the forcefulness of all that's contained within his stories bodes well for his future as an author.

His writing is passionate stuff, and it reflects an undiluted concern for our future. Because of this, I'm glad to have been able to read his writing, and I highly regard his commitment to the betterment of the species. Boring is the one thing his writing is not, and he can take justifiable pride in the knowledge that he will open the eyes of all those who get the opportunity to read him.

He presents a new clarity and—as I've said—a real force as well. The force and the personality of his prose create a special readership with the reader. again displays a distinctive voice, and I hope someday his writing will find broad expression among a mass audience. His is explosive, eloquent stuff, and the loss will belong to those who do not read it.

Scott Meredith

It conjures thoughts of Borges and Calvino.

Travis Iles

Thank you! Thank you for your gifts to the world.

E.

ani difranco's secretary

If you want to write like this, I suggest you put your writing in a drawer. Because no one will want to read it.

Abraham Verghese

What's the payoff to the reader for reading this? That I will see the light and accept your version of morality? NO WAY!

Pam Grim

I don't know what kind of sick fantasy this is, but I want no part of it.

Greg Kuhlby

Bravo, bravo, this story soars. You've written something beautiful here. I was really moved by Fracture.

Mary O'Connell

Nelson Algren Literary Award Winner

This is one of the most incredible things I have ever read, and the writing at times is better than anything I can recall. I fell into it immediately, first the poem and then the strange almost whispered beginning—an internal conversation—I was unable to stop reading. It was, as a drug, bringing me such pleasure and yet at the same time I was aware of my complete subserviance to this stack of pages in my hand. I was utterly engaged. I could not stop reading, could not put it down, for anything at all.

There is such a rhythym that is established, that I can picture, only, a pulsing light, at times there is great brightness, things are clear and real...and at other times, darkness. The moments that are 'inside' of the narrator's head are incredible. And as much as we are like the lover, I grab on to every real piece (nugget) I can get, while silently rejoicing in those internal moments, feeling bonded together with this voice, at once so wholly personal and universal. There is so much in this that is so close, and then there are things that are infinitely far away, for which I can give only sympathy, and not empathy. Amazing.

Again I am amazed by your ability to find metaphors that are able to express the complexity of this piece. It is a remarkable story, and voice, that should be allowed to speak, to sing, as long as it has the breath to do so.

Thank you. Thank you. Thank you.

Rachel Smith

Notes

House of Wonder

House of Wonder is the informal name for the Iowa International Center for Queer (Fluid) & Complex Lives. It contains a library and art museum, to date, and is a cultural and learning center for joy and **your** human possibility. It is the new prototypical educational, cultural, and spiritual institution for the emerging Age of Paradox and the coming new human species, *Homo adrians*.

There are all these museums for children. What about a museum for adults? What about a place where adults can explore their wonder and complexity and fluidity—things that are blocked off from them since day one of their lives? Men are channeled into one set of behaviors, thoughts, and expectations. Women into another. But we know now that all human attributes and potentials are open to any human individual to some extent. As children we are locked into the parochial, homogenous values of our local culture and neighborhood. But now with transhistorical and cross-cultural information all of the world's histories and cultures are open to us. It is no longer "us versus them." We have discovered them and they are us.

At the House of Wonder you finally get to meet your congruent and fully-developing self.

Would you like to support this vanguard cultural center? Annual memberships are $40. They are not tax-deductible at this point, but they support a great cause. The House of Wonder website should be operational by the end of 2000. Please look for it as you surf the Web. ***Thank you!***

www.houseofwonder.com

References

1 Kuppers

2 poem fragment, Rainer Maria Rilke

3 Gluck, p. 41

4 Beachy, p. 61

5 Verghese

6 U2

7 Bell, p. 34

8 author unknown, from a Hallmark™ greeting card

9 title and poet momentarily unknown

Bibliography

Beachy, Stephen (1994). Hunters/Gatherers. In **High Risk 2**, Amy Scholder & Ira Silverberg (eds.) New York: Plume

Bell, Marvin (1994). To Dorothy. In **A Marvin Bell Reader**. Hanover, NH: Middlebury College Press.

Gluck, Louise (1992). The Wild Iris. New York: Ecco Press.

Kuppers, Bernd-Olaf (1990). Information and the origin of life. Cambridge, MA: MIT Press.

U2 (1991). Love is blindness. **Achtung Baby.** London: Island Records.